FLASHES & FLOATERS
14 Fictions

—Conrad Bishop—

WordWorkers Press
Sebastopol CA

Contents

MAUI

I got a letter. It said OFFICIAL.

Dubious: they all try to look official, though they've just designed an envelope that looks hideously like the IRS.

But this was in fact official. NOTIFICATION OF PRIZES.

A contest I'd entered. At the Target I bought six pairs of socks, which always wore holes in a month but gave you that zing of *bargain!* A display invited me to win a trip to Hawaii, so I put a card in a box. I hated the stereotype where they hang flowers on your neck and twang ukeleles and wiggle, but my friend Bud had rhapsodized on Maui—the volcanoes, the gods, the magic.

I could use some magic. Fifty-two, divorced, thinning hair, a salesman, which made me an expert on yearning. On weekends I strive to seek meaning in life. I look like everyone else, only more so.

And the second prize was an iPhone. I could use another iPhone: blow music through my head when I'm trying not to think.

But the letter said YOU HAVE WON.

I scoured it, looking for the catch, like *Conditional upon purchase of Florida real estate.* I even read the small print, those teensy black microbes in attack formation. No, I'd won. I'd really won.

I'd never won a prize before.

So I called the number, and an actual human answered, and yes, congratulations, all I had to do was come in to arrange an all-expense-paid week in Hawaii. Not just touristy Waikiki: any place I wanted.

"Maui?"

"Sure, Maui."

So I went to the travel agency. A nice middle-aged redheaded woman was sitting there, and I gave her my confirmation number, and she said, "So where would you like to go?" and I said, "Maui."

I feared she might ask why and I'd have to mumble about volcanoes and gods and magic, which would embarrass us both, but she didn't. She motioned me to sit and got on the keyboard—"What kind of hotel? Car?"—and so on. Finally, "Okay, I'm printing out your tickets and reservations." She printed them out, handed me the envelope, and smiled. "Enjoy your stay in Omaha."

"Sorry?"

"Have a great time—"

"That's really funny: I thought you said, 'Enjoy your stay in Omaha.'"

"—Though sadly, the Stockyards are closed. People ask about that."

I looked at my ticket. It said OMAHA, NEBRASKA.

"Excuse me," I chuckled, "talk about technical glitches, I mean, but you were booking me to Maui and for some reason it printed OMAHA."

"Omaha is really undiscovered," she said.

"Well I'm sure it is, but—"

"I get that question a lot," she said. I hadn't asked her a question. "But why not give it a whirl?"

"Well, see," I said, "my letter says *Hawaii* but all these tickets you've very kindly given me say *Omaha*. Doesn't that strike you as a little bit paradoxical, kind of? A bit surprising, maybe?"

"Nothing surprises me," she said.

I wasn't sure that *paradoxical* was quite the right word, though lately I'd been using it a lot. She said that lots of Nebraskans go to Hawaii, so maybe she meant that the exodus from Omaha sucked us all into the vacuum. I'd never had physics in high school.

She was not unattractive, so we got into a chat. I said that my uncle went to Arizona to die among Republicans. She too was divorced, had this job for a couple of years, and her son was arrested recently for stealing a parking meter. We might be sprouting rapport. Then she said, "I think you'll really like Omaha." So we were back to that.

I saw that she was serious. Some ploy to save her company money? Or maybe she'd had a stroke and only remembered how to get to Omaha? Was there something in Hawaii they don't want us to know about? Conspiracy theories were ways of creating coherent reality from irreconcilable facts.

Being in sales myself, I leaned over and said gently, "You know, what I really want is I want to go to Maui. I'm sure Omaha is great and the Comfort Inn on West 72nd is unforgettable, but right now I just want to go to Maui, cause Nebraska's kinda short on volcanoes, so if you can't book me there could I talk to your supervisor?"

"My supervisor's on vacation in Hawaii."

So we went around and around, and I started to think about screaming to make my point clearer. But then she raised her finger, as if to a little boy, and with deep distant eyes murmured this: "Have you ever known someone who seems mature and very polite, college education, impeccable resume, but who is, perhaps on account of society's many flaws, insane?"

I said I believed that I had.

Like a crazed prophet from Sunday School, she fixed me with her gaze and spoke these words: "Omaha is the Heartland, and in this time of madness, we must return to the heart."

~

Omaha is really quite nice. Yesterday I went to the Henry Doorly Zoo and spent quality time with the baboons. This afternoon I take a tour out to Offutt Air Base and Boys Town, an orphanage they made a movie about. There are good steak houses, though I don't eat beef, and an art museum. And there's plenty of crime and racial tension, so it doesn't feel like some hick town.

In some ways I'm disappointed, but this may be for the best. Because Maui is a dream, and perhaps in these hours of crisis, as she said, we should rein in our dreams and keep them on hand for a brighter day. Is this sad year a time for gratification, gladness, joy?

Omaha dwells in every American's heart. We've won it. We have to go there.

BIRDS FALLING

We had just come back from vacation, I, my wife Kelly and the kids, who didn't mind missing school—a week down to San Diego to visit friends who were having a rocky time—when the birds began to fall.

They fell mostly at night, very soft plops. You could hear it if you stopped breathing. Then in the morning, nothing. Maybe the homeless eat'em, I joked, and Josh laughed, my son. We thought it must just be local.

That was in May, same time that Kelly was diagnosed and she had to go in for treatments. I drove her back and forth. Once I ran a red light, but I said I was taking my wife for treatments and he didn't write me up.

Time went on. It was in the papers now, national news, but like biohazards or climate change, it was just one of those things. It upset Kelly a lot. She cared less about herself and more about the birds.

There was all kinds of crazy news. Some blamed the current Administration. A respected dentist cited the prophecy of Isaiah. Pundits recounted evidence of vegan involvement. Intimations of fascist plots gained traction. Choose your truth.

Now they started falling at sun-up, and they'd hit like little cherry bombs. I recalled when my friend Artie, third grade, stuck a firecracker under his sleeping cat. Some people got hit really bad, so they kept the kids off the playgrounds.

I didn't pay lots of attention, though it was big news when the last Golden Eagle dropped at a shopping mall in Missoula. Our National Bird was kaput. There were calls for investigation, but Kelly was in the last stages.

Next week past the eagle thing, she died, and they nailed me for running a light. I wasn't thinking.

At the funeral, my niece Jennifer, who's four, babbled about the birds, and my sister Sandra told her, "Never mind the birds, you should be sad about Aunt Kelly. The birds, they're like dinosaurs or the Indians, they were nice but they're gone. In the Bible it says, *All things must pass.* So shut up with the birds." Jennifer cried harder, so Sandra said, "You know, maybe there's birds on the moon or in Outer Space." But Jennifer cried and the preacher looked over. I can't remember Sandra ever crying. Maybe she wanted to. Maybe she would some day.

After a month or so, it was still a risk to go out. Now they fell harder, those that were left, exploding like tiny grenades, blowing holes in the roofs of cars. I sat in the house as if stuck in Limbo with nothing to read. Some days came like waterfalls in a rush, others seeped in like syrup over pancakes. I said those things to Sandra when we went out to dinner, and she grinned. Nuff said about Sandra.

They say that all things pass. One morning in August, maybe, the birds began rising up into daylight with their shrill. I'd sit on the porch staring into the sky, hoping for something to touch and smell. I couldn't think of anything to say. I was only listening.

Birds criss-crossed the skies. Sometimes they coalesced into patterns, spelling out words as the sun moved into an autumn slant. This was a time of hope.

School started. The children learned of the Ice Age, and how it passed, how the tribes moved into new valleys and made drawings in caves of the wonders they dreamed. The children still had nightmares, then they heard the new birds at dawn and forgot all the monsters. I even imagined a time when birds would cross across in abundance, having known countless extinctions and taken them all in stride.

I remembered Kelly. Her lips.

DEATHBED

She was trying not to die. She knew she would eventually—we all did, they say—but so much depended on her holding out. She couldn't think what, but at least one day would make all the difference.

She tried to think. All the files to sort, the photos, directives for the kids. At least she'd never had kids, or had she? They might be handy to deal with it all. Like the songs.

Her songs, she knew she had songs, at least the lyrics. She wasn't sure where they came from, just stuff she sang to herself. Showed up on the porch like feral cats.

The pain? The pain was one of those pesky friends who came to visit. Friends you couldn't stand, but you had to put up with your friends. Just ask if they'd like coffee, and then you could crouch in the kitchen until they were gone.

Something inside her wanted to kill her. Her cancer had an intelligence, like the roach scurrying over the counter. We none of us want to die, not even a bug. Your legs just tell you to run.

Her children might die if she did. They were the next in line. She named them Ruth and Anthony, old-fashioned names which they would have hated, if she'd ever had kids. She'd wanted kids, but did she have them? Try to remember. Just try.

A strange man sat at the foot of the bed. His name was Earl, her husband. Earl wasn't helping things, sitting there.

"How you doing, hon?" He was asking something.

"You looked like a stranger."

"I'm not really up to it."

He was a joker. She liked that about him, though she wasn't in any mood. He always said stuff in a funny voice, so you knew it was a joke. Then you could try to laugh.

She'd woken up thinking Earl was the Devil. Why? She'd quit the church, though she liked the stories—the Nativity, the loaves and fishes—and how they said we should all be nice. But the stains hung in.

The stains, like when Earl spilled red wine on his pants. One more thing to take care of. The IV rack stood there dripping poison into her arm. And there was Earl sitting there staring with his dull tormented eyes.

She fumbled in the bedclothes for a pen, thinking to make a list if she found it. Daily tasks, directives. Or to outline her paper for freshman English. If she failed it and died, Miss Ketter would feel so guilty.

Now there was tumult and scurry. The nurses converged like a squad of Marines. She was tousled and trounced. All stuff was a ruckus outside her. Earl's face was there and then thank God he was gone.

Then silence. Earl stood at the window and looked to be weeping. He always sounded weird when he wept, but this was dead silent. It must be that she'd died. With all the havoc she'd missed it.

What next was the question. She'd heard it called a great journey, but she hated travel. If you weren't satisfied with staying home, you'd made a big mistake. Sometimes she'd longed to make a big mistake, but you had to be more attractive. The only mistake she'd made was marrying Earl, but that wasn't anyone's fault, it was more like running out of gas. At some point, someone would tell her what to do. You wouldn't have to work it out for yourself, she remembered from Sunday School. Meantime, she'd close her eyes and get some rest. They were already closed.

And then she was falling, falling, falling blind, and never hit the bottom.

IN LINE AT THE DOOR

I was standing in line. Many reasons to stand in line: to get an ice cream cone, to fill out forms, to use the porta-potty. Normally I would have known my reason for standing there. I'd known when I left the house, but the weather had been unpredictable. By the time I got up to the door I'd remember.

The line stretched down the block, circled back on itself, then back again, rounded a corner and disappeared to the west, so that once you got within sight of the door, you were heading toward it, then away, then toward it—same line, same door, but an ever-changing perspective. Far off, the line crossed a busy thoroughfare. We all had to wait till the tanks rolled past and the stoplight turned.

At the start of my trek to the end of the line, I caught a glimpse of the door. A plain black door, two white columns rising on either side, topped by Corinthian capitals, those acanthus leaves and scrolls. In high school I laughed at the Greeks putting salads and toilet rolls on top of a marble column. High school was sometimes a hoot.

The sky was a gun-metal gray, acidic, curdled, bruised. Traffic squawked and grumbled past. Drivers smirked and waved. Glad I'm not you, they were saying, but after they'd looked for a parking place, fumbled for change, concealed their valuables, locked their doors, and made the slog from wherever they parked to the end of the line, which they knew in their hearts they'd have to do, they'd hum a different tune.

I would have gone to the very end, but someone waved me: cut in here. I declined, of course, but his gesture was insistent. It was a ruddy roly-poly man in a brown fedora. My mother had warned me never to talk to roly-poly strangers, but Mom was long gone. "Thanks," I murmured, but he was less than talkative. Perhaps his mother had warned him, before she died, against tall gaunt strangers in horn-rims.

The line lurched forward. They must be letting us in by tens. Those I'd seen near the front, their faces bore no concern, or perhaps only a flicker of shadow as they strained to listen for sounds within. We were waiting forever for what we didn't know. The line lurched again. It might be sooner than I'd thought.

At least I could be sociable. I turned to the roly-poly man behind me. He wasn't there. It was a gawky string-bean lady with a melted face. Not melted like candles, more like a jack-o'-lantern left out on the steps through November, wilted and chill. My heart went out to her, but I turned my back. Another lurch to the line. Like someone sucking up a spaghetti strand.

The line doubled back, and I watched others passing in the line. A daddy pushed a baby carriage without a baby. A pimply kid shuffled by with a boom box blasting too loud to hear. I hadn't seen a boom box in years. An elderly couple, their faces like crisp yellow leaves, limped past, growing shorter as they proceeded.

A stately parade. A buxom Latina with sculpted hair, flat slit of a smile, chewing. A businessman: thick lenses, fat hands. A sexless meatball, face squeezed into a pucker. A refugee family of four, the deep-black mom with an albino blotch on her cheek. A scowling teen with a sweatshirt emblazoned WHO? ME? A sharp-chinned waddling clown in a fireman's helmet. A top-hatted female Elvis from a Dickens Fair. A stout biker-type dude with a skull shaved bald and tattooed with a skull shaved bald and tattooed. The human comedy, I marveled, all moving toward the door.

Behind the door, I imagined agents in windowed booths. They would ask to see my ID, where I came from, what was my business, my mother's maiden name. They might direct me to put my thumb on a touch screen and cough. I would need an alibi and a spotless thumb. I tried again to think what my business was. From the end of the line to the open door, we needed a purpose in mind. But what to expect? Maybe you enter and it just happens, the way they do it with hogs.

I'm near the door. I need to concentrate. I have business here, important, and this is the line. Again I try to remember why I came, but I keep thinking of the biker dude with a tattooed skull tattooed onto his tattooed skull. I've never talked with a biker dude. This might be my very last chance.

LOOT

The movers came. My husband Roy answered the door. "Jiffy Movers," they said and walked right in. Two of them, and then there were more. They looked Mexican, which was scary but maybe no sweat. Supposedly they're just people.

"What's this?" I asked one.

"Jiffy Movers," the fat one said, and they started to carry stuff in. Boxes, big heavy cardboard boxes marked Sony, Apple, Prada, Hammacher Schlemmer, Bang & Olufsen, more. Entertainment centers, microwaves, ermine bedspreads and toilet seat covers, fairy lights and terrariums. One box pictured a robotic vacuum, then a 3D printer, shapewear and a beanie hat that was making news and multi-fingered fidget spinners.

We just said, "Over there," and Roy moved the sofa to give it room. I thought at first I was dreaming, but it wasn't wispy the way they do in the movies: the stuff was real, and the edges were cold and sharp as a knife. The good life spread out before us like multifarious roadkill, although I'd never say it that way. Maybe I felt dizzy.

It kept coming for hours. I almost expected a stuffed horse or a bowling alley for the bedroom or an indoor/outdoor barbecue pit. Roy grinned when I told him that.

We were jammed chock full, every room in the house, no place to sit except the chaise longue they delivered at four p.m. "A serendipitous windfall," I said. Which didn't sound like me at all. I didn't even know what that meant. Roy looked at me like, *What?*

We signed for it all. The skinny brown man with a mustache and droopy eyes, the crew chief, I guess, said, "Muchas gracias." I knew what that meant, but not sure how he meant it.

Four-thirty our kids came home, Lainie and Max. "What's this?"

"Stuff," I said.

"Lotta stuff," Roy said.

"A panoply," I said. They looked at me like, *Mom?*

He started to unpack the boxes and do the set-ups, a noisome task indeed. There, I did it again. "You're so skilled at making things manifest," I said. Which sure didn't sound like me. I was talking like some drunk poet or something.

A crazy mistake, the whole deal, but how could we say take it back? If they said you won the Lottery, you wouldn't say, "Hey, sorry, we don't really need that ten million bucks." We deserved it as much as anyone else. Some people get born into winning, the rest of us count on luck.

Our daughter Lainie smirked, made a wisecrack about white privilege, and Roy said, "Hey, sign me up for more!" But he started to look scared.

It took weeks to unpack and get it set up, but then, in plush, climate-controlled and vibrating rooms, we watched award-winning shows, sometimes three or four at a time. We'd get the laugh track over the hip-hop over the football over the bombs. We couldn't quit our day jobs, but we never lacked for being entertained, good thing for that.

It was I that unpacked the blender. I'd never really wanted a blender, even if we all got murdered in our beds, which I said as a joke. But there it was, a blender. Like wedding silver, a preternatural beauty to it. Which didn't sound remotely like me, but nothing else did either. Weird stuff happens to your head when you're one of the plutocrats.

But the blender, I had to use it. If you don't use it you don't deserve it, my mom always said, which I guess is why you flip on the TV when you walk through the room. So I began to blend. I blended a lemon. I blended the carrots. I blended potatoes and chard and a cantaloupe. I blended everything I could get my hands on, and the moment I looked away, the cat jumped in. Was that a hassle! Wow!

Lainie and Max still showed up for dinner most days, but they slouched down deep in their iPhones and didn't come out till bedtime. They seemed happy to partake of our largesse, though they grew more distant by the day. Not so much guilt, no, but just a disharmony, dismay. Yet though we weren't as wildly entertained, we achieved a quietude that felt leading to some kind of relief. And I stopped apologizing for sounding like a highbrow.

~

The loss of Max was a total surprise. He was fine in school, and then just before Thankgiving I went into his room with the laundry.

I keep telling myself it's all a dream and I'll wake up, like they do in the old movie. I haven't yet, but I always think I might.

I was glad that Lainie took it so well.

EXPRESS BUS

Lester "Les" Pruitt sometimes took the bus to and from his work in the city—Santa Rosa to San Francisco and back, GGT 101—which stopped in San Rafael to change drivers. A two-hour trip, but he liked the chance to read or watch the digital crawler as it repeated upcoming stops—*San Pedro Rd., Ignacio Blvd.*—or the warning signs along the way—*Work Zone, Lane Blocked, Fines Doubled.* There were always little moments: a dump truck overturned or an armchair fallen into the center lane. Always something.

Coming home late Thursday, early fall, Bus #1514 pulled into the San Rafael Bus Pad, disgorged its passengers along with the driver, a short Black man who looked very worn. He had reason to. Just past San Anselmo, a stringy young guy had come down the aisle to complain that the bus was going the wrong way. "I'm heading to Vallejo," he said.

"Wrong bus. We go to Santa Rosa."

"Lemme off!"

The driver explained that he couldn't leave off passengers on the freeway. "Black-ass mother shitfucker!" the young man screamed, and variants of that sentiment. The driver pulled onto the shoulder, opened the door, pointed. The young man descended into an unscheduled future.

It broke the boredom of the trip, but the kid might have had a gun, and then it'd make the ten o'clock news. The passenger Les Pruitt wondered how many would go out and arm themselves. He wondered if he would. When the bus pulled into San Rafael, the driver was quickly gone. They all sat waiting.

Ten minutes later, an eight- or nine-year-old boy climbed the steps of the bus and wedged himself in at the wheel. Les empathized with his mom or dad: how embarrassing to lose track of your kid and undergo the stares. And the little boy, frankly, was obese. Had they allowed him to overindulge, or did they grieve at his glandular condition? Would Les's own two kids ever squeeze into a bus driver's seat? He'd never told them not to. So many things to tell them not to do.

Les noticed that the boy was dressed in brown and carried a bus driver's cap. He was not an attractive child. His deathly pale skin was sunburnt. His tiny black eyes bulged out of his face like a roly-poly rat. His fingers were little pig sausages. His hair was a duck-ass cut Les had seen in Fifties movies. His face bore infinite sadness.

Les looked out the window for the parents. New passengers came up the steps, flashed their cards or slotted their cash in the cash machine. He looked for the actual driver. Yet this boy wore the brown uniform, put on the billed hat, and appeared to feel fully authorized.

The door swung shut. The child had pushed a lever and was starting the bus. The engine growled. No way could his feet reach the pedals, but Les recalled that many new busses had hand controls. He looked to the other passengers. No one seemed concerned. A young Asian dude in red tennis shoes blasted music through his head. A gray lady touched the screen of her smart phone. A hook-beaked man read a prescription bottle. A perk-nosed brunette shut her eyes, waiting for life to pass. The bus coughed, juddered, and heaved its massive buttocks into the twilight.

No problems on the freeway, not at first. Without incident they passed shopping centers, dealerships, rolling hills, a billboard urging all to *Unite for a Drug-free World*, and then they picked up speed. The little boy stood upright behind the wheel, and then at last Les realized the obvious: it was a midget. He'd never realized before that he was biased against midgets.

At the exits they ran stop signs, crashed through a *Lane Blocked* barrier. They swerved into the Petaluma Bus Pad and swerved out again. *Redwood Boulevard* and *Olive Avenue, Detour, Shoulder Work, Graton Resort & Casino, Bella Cox for Congress.* Somehow they crossed into the on-coming lanes, headlights looming, veering off to the right or the left. Their hurtling bulk claimed right-of-way. Other drivers saw the madness a mile away and skidded into a ditch. The fat boy giggled, and then Lester Pruitt realized a greater truth: it wasn't a midget, it was a little boy.

In the bus, a wheelchair broke loose from Wheel-chair Securement, spinning a spindly Black woman down the aisle. She emitted shrill parrot shrieks. A burly man flopped into her lap to stop her, but a wiry young wom-an pummeled his head. They roared over an underpass, under an overpass. The dotted lines blended, multiplied. There were dozens of lanes, and they were in them all. The little boy steered one-handed and blew a bubble.

There comes a point in utter terror when all shudder-ing stops, when you know you're in as deep as there is to go. Like that pioneer tale Lester hated in school: the family caught in the blizzard. They kill their horse, cut it open, crawl into its warm guts and blood. The ice wind screams, but they cling together in bloody survival mode.

They weren't heading to Santa Rosa. A streak of incidents—careening off a guardrail, side-swipes, two cyclists taken out—made Les hopeful the cops were on the way. He prayed that someone might stop the child, take him home, kill him, whatever. The boy had been flashing the headlights on and off, but now, near midnight, he must be gunning it up past ninety in total dark. At times a passenger cried out or whimpered to no effect. Lester's wife must be calling friends. He begin to think how he'd lived his life and what he'd like to change. He prayed for the bus to run out of gas or crash into a culvert or hit a truck, but it only howled faster and faster into the night.

TWO TRAINS

IMAGINE TWO TRAINS LEAVE FOR OMAHA, SAME TIME, AT 80 MPH. ONE GOES FROM DENVER, HAULING CATTLE. WHEN WILL THEY MEET?

I read over this many times. Algebra was fifth period, when I always got sleepy, so I had a hard time watching the X jump back and forth over the equals sign. But this was the mid-term, a quarter of the grade. If you scored high, you went to college and got the girl and all the good things of life. If not, you forever washed your clothes in the laundromat.

The teacher dozed at his desk. He was young, asked us to call him Mister Bob, which struck my parents, when I told them, as a disrespect of authority. But would I disrespect him more by following his request or by saying "Mister Nolan"? I addressed him as "Scuse me…" so the issue was moot.

I'd learned the word *moot* from debate club, and it was comforting—the sense that we're past the point when action is relevant, so there's nothing to do, so it's fine to stop obsessing because we're already screwed.

But this problem wasn't moot. Its claws were on my neck. I went up to the desk.

"Scuse me?"

He stirred. "Yes?"

"This problem. There must be a typo. Wouldn't we have to know the mileage for both, and when they start out?"

"That's part of the problem."

"But it can't be answered, can it?"

He looked at the paper in puzzlement. At last he raised his eyes to me as if he saw my long path ahead and how ill-prepared I was for the journey.

"There's lots of things, Raymond, that perplex us. This is the least of what's in store."

"But I don't see it's possible to find the answer. Not with algebra."

"Algebra is only a tool."

"But this is algebra class."

He nodded in sympathy with my concerns, kept nodding as his eyelids drifted to half-staff.

I went back to my desk, skipped over the puzzler. The other problems were no sweat, but this one was in all-caps—did that mean it carried more credit? I thought of asking Mister Bob, but he was snoring softly.

During tests, we were allowed to wander around, copy others' answers, ask friends for help. "All life is interdependent," he had said, "but it's for you to decide whose truth you trust." I meandered up and down the aisles, noticing that all my classmates had made sallies at the two trains, only to skip to the next.

The last paper I checked was Darrell's, the class dummy. Darrell had pimples, bad teeth, and was way overweight, but he was the only one with an answer, though with not a trace of calculation: *8:40 p.m.* I copied it. Turned out he didn't get any other problems right, but I aced the mid-term.

I was glad the trains arrived.

KILLING JAMES

College at last. For Intro to Econ 101, we were assigned to do "collaboration." The prof was young, told jokes, and was very well-liked—until then.

The idea was to introduce us to interdependence. In the real world, he called it, you never worked alone. Even poets interacted with their editors, their publishers, the cover designer, the publicist, colleagues who'd promote them, and rich spouses who'd support them. Even a billionaire entrepreneur needed a ballsy secretary who could tell him he was being an asshole. We all said *asshole* routinely, but it still sounded strange from a prof.

"So you'll select a topic for your term paper and write it in collaboration. Groups of three. Count off." We divided into threes, with one disgruntled foursome.

"What about grades?" someone asked.

"You're all in it together. Welcome to real life."

A chorus of groans, and a few kids came up with arguments against the concept—cogent but ineffective. *Welcome to real life* carried the day. Added attraction: he would grade on a curve, each trio competing with the others. "Life is competition, sad to say." The prof in fact looked griefstricken at his ethical obligation to crucify his students.

Choosing the term paper topic was a breeze. Chloe was our trio's female alpha male: short, blonde hair clipped into a helmet, pixie piranha face with a slash of blood-tinted lipstick over a plastic smile, and bullet tits. Her ambition was to be CEO of a major cosmetics company—she already had her articles of incorporation—so our topic would be "The Economics of Maquillage." I had to look that up, and I feared it might be somewhat ambitious for a freshman intro class, but it was hard to withstand Chloe's basilisk stare. James never said a word.

And through most of the semester, our assigned co-hort James never said a word, except sometimes "Okay" in a trembly birdlike voice that matched his runt face. James just sat there, gave off a mild stink of terror and scratched his head a lot. He might have bird lice, I thought, and a huge hairy brute of a dad.

Given James' unprepossessing physique and retiring air, one might expect that he had intellectual gifts that would soar us above the rabble. We had heard endless sermons, through preschool, grade school, high school, and greet-the-frosh blurts, that we were each of us special, that quadriplegics were other-abled, that everyone had a gift. This did not stand up to scrutiny. James, despite his other deficiencies, was lazy and stupid.

This might have smoothed our so-called collaboration: James would be ignored and I would take orders from Chloe—I had no problem with female hegemony if it bettered my grade-point. But we had to keep a journal on interpersonal dynamics, our capacity to elicit contributions from everyone involved, and not even Chloe was fully skilled—as yet—in the art of blatant lies: that was a senior-level seminar. James' existence would drag down our leaky boat.

Mid-semester, we decided to kill James.

It was Chloe's suggestion, of course, and I raised some delicate concerns—the death penalty, for example, not to mention an F in Intro. But she came up with a convincing business plan. She would flirt with James, arrange to meet him in the secluded Shakespeare Garden, which served as a collegiate lovers' grove. I would check nearby couples to make sure they wouldn't notice, and as James quivered birdlike in Chloe's lock-jaw kiss, I would come up and bop him.

So that's what we did. He was found a day later by a gay couple, who were quickly convicted of the deed. As his friends we were questioned, of course, but investigations slacked off once they'd beaten confessions from the gays.

I finished the project with Chloe, and we got a B+. The prof was a very tough grader, despite his jocular nature. No one ever got an A in an intro course—those were designed to instill a lasting sense of deficiency. Yet Chloe went on to achieve her cherished ambition, and I managed okay.

~

Years later, I ran into the young professor, no longer young, at the hotel bar of a convention in Des Moines. We got to talking about the ancient tragedy of James, and he expressed a degree of guilt for such a rough assignment. I assured him it was very productive. "It was real," I said.

And I had my own nightmares, of course, which diminished over the years. My MBA studies included a required course, Business Ethics. At the outset the prof joked about its being an oxymoron, but we'd heard it a million times.

And I recently heard an interview on NPR. A best-selling shrink made the point that if we felt our world falling apart, we'd be up for anything. We'd grab for money, for the last available seat, for the handgun, for the Fuehrer. Indeed, he spoke true. In those undergrad days, we sensed our world falling apart before we'd even stuck it together.

But I'd already forged my own rationalization, as humans are wont to do. First, as Chloe said, it was nothing new: it happens every day. And poor James was lucky that we spared him an inevitable life of pain. And the assignment's whole point was to give us a taste of real life. If we'd had the guts to come clean about it, we might have scored an A.

LOSING IT

My name, I'm quite sure, is Millard Foote. As long as I can remember it. But this morning I couldn't find my cup of tea. I'd brewed it five minutes ago, trying again with the herbal stuff, which tasted like licking paper, but if I let it steep and put my nose close down to the cup, I could smell an orangey tang. Caffeine made me fart. That gets me cranky.

And my granddaughter's birthday was coming up. She was a thousand miles away and hadn't yet been born, but I didn't want to send bad vibes. We send messages on the astral plane, my daughter said, so I wanted no role in the baby's future neuroses. When she popped into life, she'd be on her own recognizance, so it had to be herbal tea.

I had set the cup on the kitchen counter while I shaved, but it wasn't there. I checked the shelf by the radio: no cup. I looked in the cabinet, on the chance that I'd reshelved it. A half dozen cups, one with a Yankees logo, one with obscene penguins, one proclaiming *Milwaukee!*—but none full of tea. I sighed. I wasn't senile, only forgetful. You don't do that much damage by what you forget; it's what you remember to do.

I scanned the living room, the study, went back to the bedroom to check if I might see myself lying unmade in the bed. No: only a tortured pillow, the covers in Gordian knotwork. In the mirror I stood in my plaid flannel shirt with no pants, only boxer shorts and heavy wool socks. At least I stood on my own two feet, the way Americans stand if they love their country and aren't wearing pants.

Another trip through the house, but no stray cup, no pants, no clue. Sometimes I joked to my dentist, a perky young twerp, that the elves hid my dentures, my glasses, my credit cards, though I didn't believe in elves. Still, science was springing surprises. Last week they discovered an ancient fossil, this baggy blob with a toothy mouth and no rectum. An ancestor to humans, they said. I could believe it, so why not elves?

My head was doing backflips. By now I doubted I'd ever made the tea. I'd better put on my pants. I looked around: no pants.

This old man whose name was surely Millard Foote, as I recalled from my tax returns, felt a flush of panic. It'd be like those dreams where I was back in school naked, crouched low so the algebra teacher wouldn't call me up to the board. I've read that everyone has this pantsless dream, but looking around the classroom I was the only one. I wondered if in strippers' dreams they worried about having no pants or more about the algebra.

One thing after another: where the hell was my algebra book? They never said what to do if you lost it.

I must have blacked out, as I often did remembering school. I found myself out on the porch, barefoot, bare-legged, snowflakes dandruffing down, and I'd shed my plaid flannel shirt. I should check in the pickup—1990 Silverado, a faded blue—for my tea or my pants or my algebra book. My daughter had asked, "What kind of color is that?" "Blue," I said. She seemed satisfied with that and soon got pregnant, I couldn't remember exactly when, the calendar having fallen behind the stove. No great loss, as most of the days were already gone, and the telephone also had disappeared. I still kept the pad to write down the calls that never came.

The Silverado was parked in the drive. Or I thought it was. It was gone—the Chevy Silverado that the previous owner used to haul potatoes. He said if I ever wanted to sell it, it was a proven potato-hauler. I myself rarely hauled a potato, but without the Silverado, I'd have to haul my potatoes by hand, one by one with no pants. And potatoes inflamed my joints.

No pickup, no pants, no potato, and where was that goddamned herb tea? My name was Millard Foote, no question, none, but I had no way to prove it. I stretched my shivering hands to my granddaughter a thousand miles away, but she was still considering being born, weighing the pros and cons.

I sighed, turned back to the house for another search, and found the door was locked. Somehow I knew that was coming. I jiggled it, felt in my pocket for keys: no keys, no pockets, no pants. The neighbors were on vacation, and I couldn't knock pantslessly on a stranger's dsoor. I'd have to walk into town to make a call to ask to let myself in, if someone was there to answer the absent telephone. It might be miles.

I had known this trip was coming but had hoped to see my daughter's new girl. I walked down the icy pathway, I being very possibly Millard Foote. The snow fell gently about me like fairy dust.

Right now I could use that cup of tea.

CHECKERS

Reg and Marg played checkers on alternate Tuesdays. Reg saw the chiropractor, Marg made her library trip, then they met at the Senior Center. Neither cared for the game, but it passed the time. That's a man's game, old Victor joked, forgetting he'd said it every Tuesday.

They rarely finished a game. Reg would complain of music that Marg couldn't hear, or Marg's leg cramp cramped. And they both had cats to feed.

Words emerged between them like bubbles or dandelion fluff or dead guppies rising up to the surface, glittering a moment, then winking out. They held perfectly still, watching their hands make the moves. Neither could tell who spoke.

—You'd think they'd know better.

—Yes you would. Who?

—You'd think so, but they don't.

—Course not. Your move.

A couple of moves. Somebody looked into the room, then disappeared. People did that. They'd both lost friends that year.

—One doesn't ever know better.

—Who?

—They know, but they don't know better.

—Your move.

The outside lobby door opened. Traffic noise spilled over the furnace rumble.

—You know what she said? She said it was what we did. When she was little, so she couldn't ever get happy. Sometime we told her no when that wasn't the right thing to say, so she had to go stick her head in the oven.

—Not for me she didn't.

—Nor for me. Your move.

Move. Jump. Jump. The furnace huffed off, but a radio played some screechy thing. They tried to hear who was speaking.

—Or my second boy. He told me, he said, It's the soldiers. Little toy soldiers we got him. He liked to play with the soldiers. He said, If I get shot it's because of the soldiers.

—Well he did.

—But was it because of the soldiers?

—Your move.

A move, a move, a move, a jump. The checkers lined up to die.

—I didn't want it.

—Neither did I.

—It just happened.

—And the oldest—

Who was it now? Who spoke? Their eyes met. Reg tilted her head to the side. What did she mean by that? Which of them wondered about what which of them meant?

—The oldest. Walter, was it? He'd babble out all the latest reports. The car wasn't safe. The bomb was dirty. People died from the yolks of eggs. You didn't have to be born. All that.

—They never learn to stop crying. They only learn to talk.

—He stopped.

—If you could call it that.

A pause in the game. They looked at the board. Who was white, who was red?

—Your move.

—It's yours.

—Well, what?

It's a man's game, old Victor had joked. Yes it was. All about killing.

—But what can they ask? We had to live. It was all a slap in the face. One slap in the face after another, just to live. What can they ask?

—But it hurts to think we're to blame.

—We're not.

—But it hurts to think it.

—Yours.

Reg felt her spine edging out of adjustment, and Marg knew the books she'd just borrowed were already overdue. They made their moves, and a jump when they couldn't avoid it. Marg thought the rules required you to jump when you could, but they came to no conclusion. Whatever happened would happen.

—What can we do?

—What?

—What?

—We could forget.

It takes two to tango, the song went. Tango, tangle. Each of them thought she was speaking now.

—When they were young, we dressed them in all the softest things. We even changed the detergent. We taught them manners. We taught good and bad, and they got candy when they were good. We sacrificed. All the sleepless nights, all the saying things over and over. They had their dumplings on their plate. Thanksgiving, Christmas, Easter, Memorial Day, the Fourth of July. Year after year.

—Every damn year.

—And then one day they looked up from the plate and they said, We're dead. Mommy, Daddy, we're dead. We said, No dear, you're not, it's just a phase, eat your peas. We can't eat our peas, we're dead. We said, We're not to blame, it was all the TV, all the noise. They said, We don't care about that. We're dead. And we said, Just wait, just wait till you have kids, then you'll see. And they said, We'll still be dead.

—You know what mine said? I'm a birthday candle, Mama. Blow me out.

❧

Both had kings. The kings were at diagonal corners of the board. They moved them back and forth.

—But there's always the hopes.

—Oh yes, the hopes.

—And grandchildren. You have lovely grandchildren.

—So do you. Except for them.

Reg went into a coughing fit. Marg replied with a concurring cough. Then a span of silence over the face of the checkerboard.

—Otherwise we could forget.

—Otherwise. Your move.

—Yours.

The afternoon stretched. Each woman had a single king left, confronting one another, mid-board, back and forth, back and forth, back and forth. At last they declared a truce, and each went home to her cat.

RAIN

As predicted, the rains came. It rained and it rained and it rained and it rained and it rained. I listened all night to the roof tattoo, and when at seven a.m. my alarm went blip, I dragged up to peer out the window. Solid rain. I'd call in sick.

Then I recalled: this was the day that would set me free. I'd resolved to roar into the office, confront my supervisor, speak truth to power, and slam the door. I saw Mr. Bottoms shrinking behind his teakwood desk, clutching his *Mr. Bottoms* nameplate. Now I'd have to postpone my emancipation.

I drank coffee while scanning the flat-screen. My whole life was a flat-screen now, and I longed for some curvature. I ought to feel grateful: no wives, no kids, no beagles, and today I'd intended to quit my job, but who wants to pull off a jailbreak in a tempest?

The news anchor gave the deluge a positive spin. It might lessen the crime rate or boost Web sales. It might drown illegal migrants. It was raining worldwide, so it might bog down major wars.

I checked my tweets—a deluge, a torrent, a monsoon of tweets on the rain. One of my friends, fat-nosed Jerry the Joker, tweeted *Tweet*. Another tweeted *I told you so!*

but left it at that. One blamed it on climate change, while another accused the Democrats.

I needed to go to the bathroom. The toilet was running over, so I peed in the sink. Since childhood I'd wanted to do that but never did. The day had come at last.

As a toddler, my mother said, I'd run forth madly, gleeful till I fell on my face. Grown, I deemed it safer to blend imperceptibly into the scenic background. Yet now I held to the heart of my resolution: today, somehow, my life would change. I had already peed in the sink.

I should check my food supply. Boiled potatoes in the fridge, leftover chicken, and the freezer was full of frozen peas. In the closet I had countless rolls of toilet paper, all I'd need to the age of ninety. I smiled at the thought of flinging a roll at Mr. Bottoms.

The tatter of rain was rats over broken glass. Odd: I was no poet, though in third grade I'd had to write a poem. *Frogs eat mosquitoes*, I wrote, and my mother helped me rhyme it. But now my mother was dead and my mind had gone dark. *Rats over broken glass.* I jerked myself back into 8:37 a.m.

9:20. Again, I scanned my tweets, my gurgles and blurts. Check the news, but the flat-screen was like a goldfish bowl, water creeping up the side-bar. I looked out the window, the street was a lake: a floating porta-potty, a policeman's hat, and feral cats swimming downtown. I saw neighbors on rooftops that crumbled like wet cookies, and cars were adrift with families of four.

10:15 a.m. I felt an unrooted sensation: my bungalow had come unmoored, and the water was up to my knees. I stood on the kitchen step-stool, watching toys float past from children I'd never fathered: fragments of Barbies, plastic G.I. Joes, dead robots, deflated footballs. My brain had lost its mind. I tried to remember how to think.

It rained for forty days and forty nights, then went on raining hard—on major airports, daycare centers, nail salons, churches clogged with repentant sinners, and on war-torn lands that I had never heard of. The poor clung to driftwood, the middle class scored motorboats, while billionaires bought aircraft carriers, lived for a time in luxury, and then succumbed to scurvy.

I imagined the Angel of Death, in a yellow slicker and holding a black umbrella, stopping all traffic so I alone could cross. I recalled years ago in Sunday School that God had promised not to send another flood, but talk is cheap. I wished that I believed in God so I could hold Him accountable.

The authorities tweeted that no one should venture out till the dove had found a mountaintop with an olive tree. I could hear voices among the firmament's thunder: Presidents, activists, hits from the Sixties, memories no one was old enough to have. I saw flashes of sunlight on windshields.

The heavens had sucked up five thousand years of sinners peeing in the sink and rained it down on our heads.

11:16 a.m. In the bathroom again, I slipped out of my sodden slippers, and floodwaters whirled them away. I turned on the bathtub faucet, climbed into the tub. The water rose, and I felt embraced. Indeed, my life was changing.

I was back with my third-grade class on our trip to the aquarium. Other kids were transfixed by the great slabby fish with monkey-wrench jaws, but I found a tiny window where I saw the Leafy Sea Dragon floating among the sprouts. Long whimsical protrusions fluttered out from its heart, a tender bouquet of diaphanous foliage. As I watched the fluid creature, I felt my hands, my lips, my

eyelids wavering, dissolving, leafing in Time's liquescence.
I could only sit naked in my tepid tub and weep and weep
and weep and weep and weep.

ASHES

Joellen was sitting in the coffee shop at a corner seat, waiting to pick up her husband from his eye appointment. She saw a short chunky woman come in and order, put milk in her coffee, then stop at her table.

—Is that your newspaper there?

—Be my guest.

And Joellen normally avoided conversations with strangers, but—

—So when are you due?

A mistake. The woman explained that she'd gained a lot of weight in her first pregnancy, more in the second, and still hadn't regained her figure.

—Oh God, I'm sorry. That was dumb.

—No problem. I'm Millie. It's crowded, could I sit here?

—Sure. So, two kids?

—Just one.

The woman's lips clenched, then she sat down and let it spill out, as if not wanting to talk but needing to. Other voices faded in and out: a business deal on a cellphone, two kids talking movies, someone's vacation plans.

~

So this is the way it went…

I was expecting our first child. It was a difficult and fragile pregnancy. For most of it I had to stay at home in bed. My husband Jerry took good care.

—How do you feel, hon?

—Better today, I think.

—Tea?

—No, thanks.

We had a fireplace in the bedroom, and during that span, the swallows came back to build their nests in the chimney. They'd come there a couple of years ago and kept coming back, and of course we didn't use it then, but I felt a kinship, hearing their preparations for nesting, same time as I felt my son kicking inside me.

—You feel it, Jerry?

—Lot of activity there.

—And hear the birds?

But my son lived only four days. I knew there were problems, but I didn't know how bad. They told me he'd never see, or speak, or walk, or know himself, and I had to decide whether to remove life support.

—It's your decision, Millie. Look, I'm sorry to put the whole thing on you, but he's been with you, in your body, so you're the one to say—

—Stop. Please just stop!

—Okay.

— No, I'm sorry… I want to let him go. Yes?

—Yes.

I'd had surgery, so when I got home I was still in bed. And now I could hear the swallows attending their young. I couldn't read or sleep or watch TV, I could only hear the chirping. And little kids' voices mixed in with the birds.

I had complications. I was mostly in bed for three weeks and pretty shaky. Then the young swallows flew and the parents left the nest. I thought, well, thank you, have a nice life, I'll miss your chirps. But thank God they were gone. It was all I could stand.

Sudden quiet. Such blessed relief. Then a flutter.

One of the young didn't leave. It fell into a little space between the metal liner and the fireplace brick. I could hear it bumping and floundering. It couldn't struggle free.

—You want me to do something about that?

—I don't know.

—I can give it a try.

—I don't know, I don't know, I don't know!

Then I said okay. Okay, Jerry, do something.

He wasn't sure he could do it, the liner was incredibly heavy, took hours of scraping and cracking and grunts, destroying the hearth in the process. But he managed.

—So the bird is back in the back, I can reach it, so what should I do?

—Let me.

—Careful.

I reached in past the ashes and scooped up the young bird. Weak flutter, not even a flutter, a quiver. Jerry helped me outside and I placed it on a low tree branch by the porch, the young bird, where it might be safe till it got up strength to fly.

Next morning it still clung to the branch. I sat on the step and watched. The sun came out and touched it. In a while, it ruffled its feathers, then it stretched its wings and it flew. I couldn't believe it was strong enough, but it flew.

I felt in that moment, in the morning light, that I'd done the right thing, allowing my son to die. He had been trapped in the dark, no way to fly, and I had set him free.

❧

Joellen wondered what she could say that didn't sound dumb. Maybe enough that she listened. She too had lost a child but never spoke of it.

—So… Yes… My boy was six, and he wandered off at a picnic to wade in the river. People all around, and nobody noticed.

—Omigod…

—So but maybe I'm drawn to talk with pregnant women, maybe think about trying at my age to be pregnant again.

There was a silence between them. Was it harder to lose a child you had memories of, a child you could hear saying *Mama*, or never to hear it say *Mama*? At last Millie spoke.

—Well but I have a daughter now. It was a bedfast pregnancy again, but my daughter lived. I've regained some of my shape, mostly, I like to think, but, well… My daughter's two, and she gives me a workout. I'll tell her about her brother when she's older.

Millie got up to go.

—So. Well. Good talking.

—Yes. Thanks.

Millie started to go, then hesitated. A couple passed with a toddler.

—And I keep Joseph's ashes—we named him—I keep his ashes in a small sealed box, beautiful Oriental box, and I don't actually think of him much, except when I'm gardening or lying in bed upstairs, hearing the swallows. The swallows are in the chimney again, so we don't use the fireplace now.

9 798985 683509